THE WEDDING DRESS COLORING BOOK

For

Black Girls

The Wedding Dress Coloring Book
For Black Girls

Developed and designed by Karen Brewer
Illustrations by Karen Brewer

ISBN: 9798389368927

Color Test Page

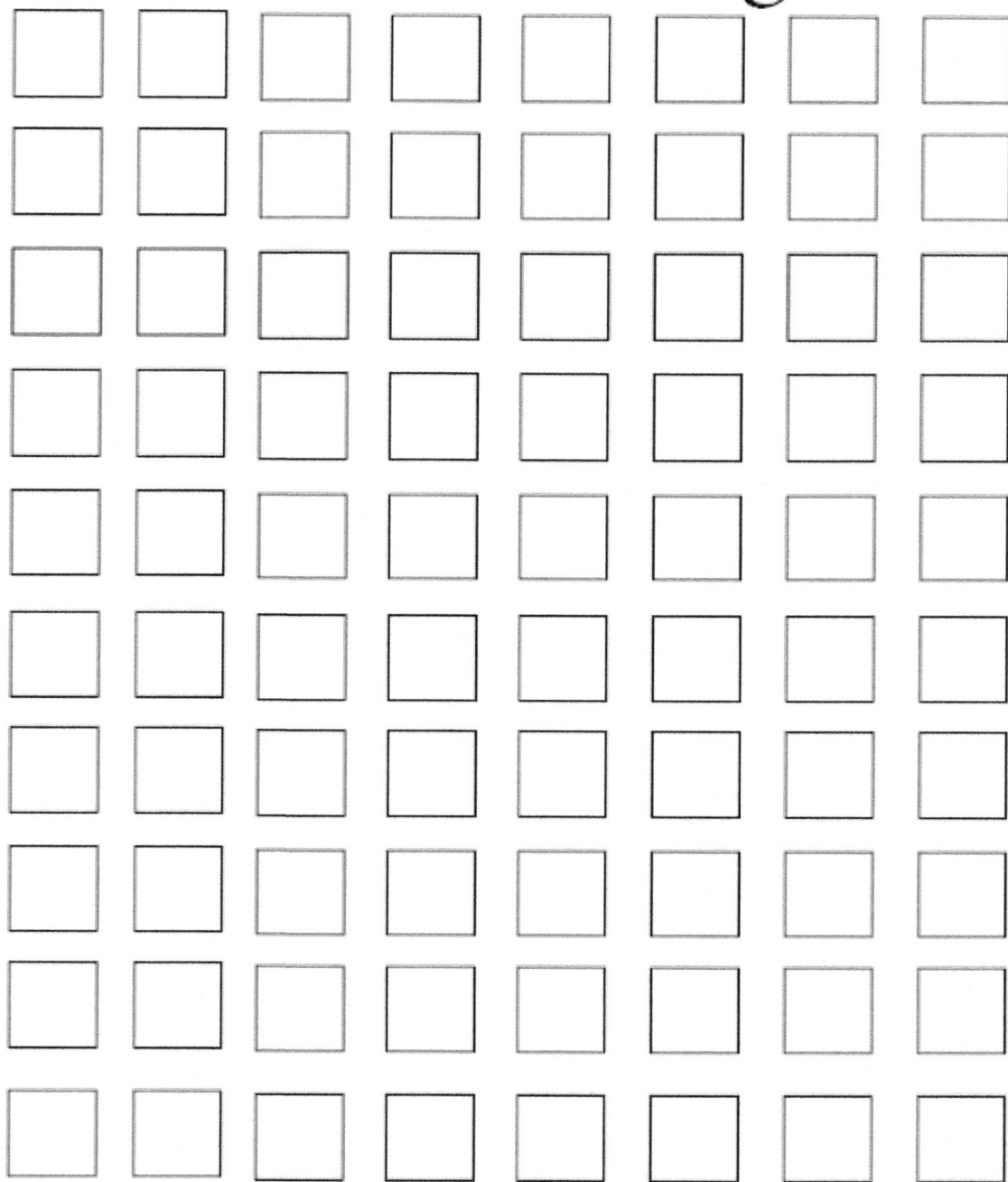

The Wedding Dress Coloring Book
For Black Girls

This book belongs to

_____

_____

_____